For information address Disney • Lucasfilm Press,
1101 Flower Street, Glendale, California 91201.

Printed in China
First Hardcover Edition, July 2016   10 9 8 7 6 5 4 3 2

ISBN 978-1-4847-8702-1
FAC-023680-17198

Visit the official *Star Wars* website at: www.starwars.com
This book was printed on paper created from a sustainable source.

STAR WARS®

The Hero's Journey Begins

Disney | LUCASFILM
P R E S S

Los Angeles • New York

Book One

A long time ago in a galaxy far, far away, a young boy named Luke Skywalker dreamed of becoming a pilot and flying into outer space. Instead, he was stuck on the desert planet Tatooine helping his uncle and aunt on their moisture farm. It wasn't exactly the exciting life Luke had dreamed of.

Little did Luke know when he joined his uncle Owen to purchase some droids from a group of Jawas, his life was about to change forever.

Luke and his uncle were looking for a droid that could speak many languages. "I'll take this one," Owen said, pointing to the golden protocol droid known as C-3PO. Luke also looked at a couple of astromech droids. At C-3PO's recommendation, Luke's uncle bought a small blue and white droid named R2-D2.

Back at home, Luke cleaned the droids and complained that he would never get off the planet. "You boys look like you've seen a lot of action," he said to the droids.

"With all we've been through, sometimes I'm amazed we're in as good condition as we are," C-3PO explained, "what with the Rebellion and all."

Luke's face lit up. "The Rebellion against the Empire?" he asked.

Just then, Luke accidentally activated a hologram, which projected from R2-D2. The image was of a young woman named Princess Leia. "Help me, Obi-Wan Kenobi. You're my only hope," her message repeated over and over again.

R2 beeped that the message was private and meant for a man named Obi-Wan Kenobi. Luke wondered if the person was related to "Old Ben" Kenobi, a strange hermit who lived in the nearby mountains.

Later, Luke told his aunt and uncle that he was worried the droid they bought had been stolen and might belong to Old Ben Kenobi.

"That wizard's just a crazy old man," his uncle said. He wanted Luke to take the droids into town the next day and have their memories erased. Luke got curious when his uncle hinted that Obi-Wan had known Luke's father. But Owen refused to talk about it.

When Luke returned to finish cleaning the droids, he discovered R2-D2 was gone! C-3PO confessed that the droid had left to find Obi-Wan Kenobi. It was too dangerous to go after him at night, so C-3PO and Luke had to wait until the next morning.

As soon as Tatooine's two suns rose, the pair took off in Luke's landspeeder. They raced across the barren landscape, tracking the droid on their scanner.

They followed R2's signal up into the rocky hills, far beyond the Skywalker farm. "Where do you think you're going?" Luke asked when they caught up to the little droid. But as they began to head back, R2 started beeping frantically.

"There are several creatures approaching," C-3PO translated.

"Sand People," Luke said. "Let's go and have a look."

They didn't get far before they were attacked by the hostile Tusken Raiders. Luke was caught off guard and knocked unconscious!

Scared, R2-D2 hid behind some rocks. The strange Sand People seemed to want to harm his friends. They were raiding Luke's landspeeder when a cloaked figure appeared over the hill, making strange sounds. The Tusken Raiders were scared away. But was the new person a friend or another attacker?

The hooded figure leaned over Luke's body. R2 was worried, until the figure pulled down the hood to reveal the face of a smiling old man. "Come here, my little friend—don't be afraid," he said to R2.

The kind old man helped Luke sit up.

"Ben Kenobi? Boy, am I glad to see you," Luke said groggily. He told the man about R2's message and asked if Old Ben was related to Obi-Wan Kenobi.

"Obi-Wan?" the old man said with a wry smile. "Now, that's a name I've not heard in a long time."

"You know him?" Luke asked.

"Of course I know him. He's *me*," the old man replied.

Luke and the droids followed Obi-Wan back to his home, where the old man told Luke more about his past.

"I was once a Jedi Knight, the same as your father," Obi-Wan said, remembering. "He was the best star pilot in the galaxy, and a cunning warrior." The old man paused before continuing, "And he was a good friend. Which reminds me, I have something here for you. Your father wanted you to have this when you were old enough." Obi-Wan handed Luke his father's lightsaber.

"What is it?" Luke asked as he instinctively ignited the glowing blue blade.

"This is the weapon of a Jedi Knight. An elegant weapon for a more civilized age," Obi-Wan said. "For over a thousand generations, the Jedi Knights were the guardians of peace and justice in the Old Republic. Before the dark times, before the Empire."

Luke was curious. "How did my father die?" he asked.

"A young Jedi named Darth Vader helped the Empire hunt down and destroy the Jedi Knights. He betrayed and murdered your father. Vader was seduced by the dark side of the Force."

Luke listened and tried to follow along, but he wanted to know more. "The Force?" he asked.

"The Force is what gives a Jedi his power," Obi-Wan explained. "It's an energy field created by all living things. It binds the galaxy together."

Back on Tatooine, Luke reminded Obi-Wan about the important message for him. Just as Obi-Wan was about to inspect R2-D2, the droid began playing the message. The hologram spoke: "General Kenobi, years ago you served my father in the Clone Wars. Now he begs you to help him in his struggle against the Empire."

The rest of the message explained that secret information—vital to the Rebellion—was stored in R2-D2. It needed to be taken to the distant planet Alderaan. It was up to Obi-Wan to help!

Obi-Wan asked Luke to join him, but Luke said no. He was already in enough trouble with his uncle for being gone so long.

"You must do what you feel is right," Obi-Wan said.

Luke offered to take Obi-Wan to the nearest spaceport. But on their way, the pair ran into the wreckage of the Jawas' sandcrawler. After a close look, Obi-Wan realized the sandcrawler had been attacked by Imperial stormtroopers.

"But why would Imperial troops want to slaughter Jawas?" Luke wondered aloud. Then he realized—they were looking for the droids! "That would lead them back . . . home!" Luke cried out.

Luke jumped into the landspeeder and rushed home. But it was too late. The Skywalker farm had been destroyed, and his aunt and uncle had been killed.

"There is nothing you could have done, Luke, had you been there,"
Obi-Wan said, trying to console the boy.

Luke was angry. But he was also determined. "I want to come with
you to Alderaan," he said to Obi-Wan. "There's nothing here for me
now." Luke took a deep breath. "I want to learn the ways of the Force and